For Dayton and Kai—
always remember the view from the backseat!

PHILOMEL BOOKS
A division of Penguin Young Readers Group.
Published by The Penguin Group. • Penguin Group (USA)
Inc., 375 Hudson Street, New York, NY 10014, U.S.A. • Penguin
Group (Canada), 90 Eglinton Avenue East, Suite 700, Toronto, Ontario M4P
2Y3, Canada (a division of Pearson Penguin Canada Inc.). • Penguin Books Ltd, 80
Strand, London WC2R 0RL, England. • Penguin Ireland, 25 St. Stephen's Green, Dublin
2, Ireland (a division of Penguin Books Ltd). • Penguin Group (Australia), 707 Collins Street,
Melbourne, Victoria 3008, Australia (a division of Pearson Australia Group Pty Ltd). • Penguin
Books India Pvt Ltd, 11 Community Centre, Panchsheel Park, New Delhi–110 017, India. • Penguin
Group (NZ), 67 Apollo Drive, Rosedale, Auckland 0632, New Zealand (a division of Pearson New
Zealand Ltd). • Penguin Books South Africa, Rosebank Office Park, 181 Jan Smuts Avenue, Parktown North
2193, South Africa. • Penguin China, B7 Jiaming Center, 27 East Third Ring Road North, Chaoyang District,
Beijing 100020, China. • Penguin Books Ltd, Registered Offices: 80 Strand, London WC2R 0RL, England.
Copyright © 2013 by Floyd Cooper. All rights reserved. • This book, or parts thereof, may not be reproduced
in any form without permission in writing from the publisher, Philomel Books, a division of Penguin Young
Readers Group, 345 Hudson Street, New York, NY 10014. Philomel Books, Reg. U.S. Pat. & Tm. Off. The scanning,
uploading and distribution of this book via the Internet or via any other means without the permission of the
publisher is illegal and punishable by law. Please purchase only authorized electronic editions, and do not
participate in or encourage electronic piracy of copyrighted materials. Your support of the author's rights
is appreciated. The publisher does not have any control over and does not assume any responsibility for
author or third-party websites or their content. • Published simultaneously in Canada. Manufactured
in China by South China Printing Co. Ltd. • Edited by Tamra Tuller. Design by Amy Wu. Text set
in 18-point Maiandra GD. • Paintings were created using a subtractive process. The medium is
mixed media. • Library of Congress Cataloging-in-Publication Data • Cooper, Floyd. • Max
and the tag-along moon / Floyd Cooper. • p. cm. • Summary: When Max leaves his
grandfather's house, the moon follows him all the way home, just as Granpa
promised it would. • [1. Moon—Fiction 2. Grandfathers—Fiction.]
I. Title. • PZ7.C78485Max 2012 • [E]—dc23 • 2011049784
ISBN 978-0-399-23342-5
1 3 5 7 9 10 8 6 4 2

Max and the Tag-Along Moon

PHILOMEL BOOKS
An Imprint of Penguin Group (USA) Inc.

Floyd Cooper

ne night, as Max was leaving Granpa's
house, he reached up to give Granpa a big
hug good-bye. In the sky behind Granpa appeared
a big fine moon.

"Look, Granpa, the moon!"

"That ol' moon will always shine for you . . .
on and on!"

Granpa and Max gazed quietly at the big moon
together as it embraced them in soft yellow light.

Max smiled at the moon and Granpa, then climbed into the car.

"Bye-bye, Granpa! Bye-bye, moon!"

As the car pulled away, Max kept his eyes on Granpa until he disappeared from sight, and all he saw was the moon.

Max kept his eyes on that moon, waiting for it to disappear, too.

The long ride home was
swervy-curvy. This way
and that, all the way.
And the moon seemed
to tag along.

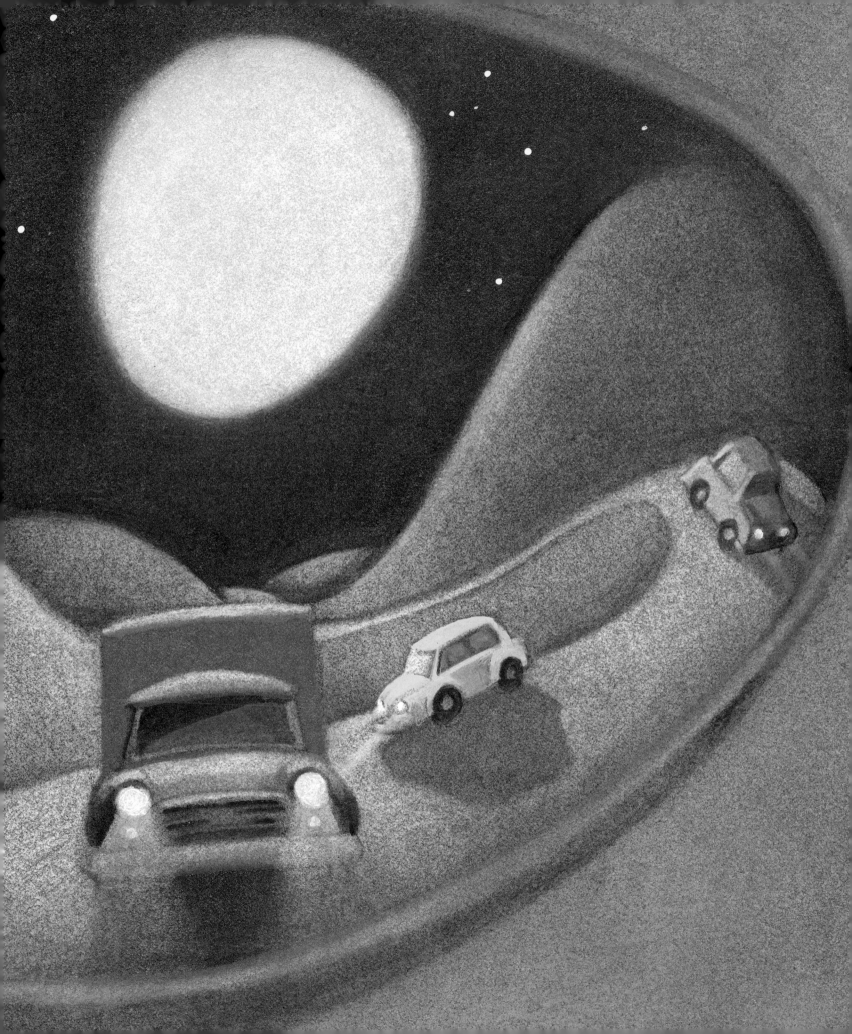

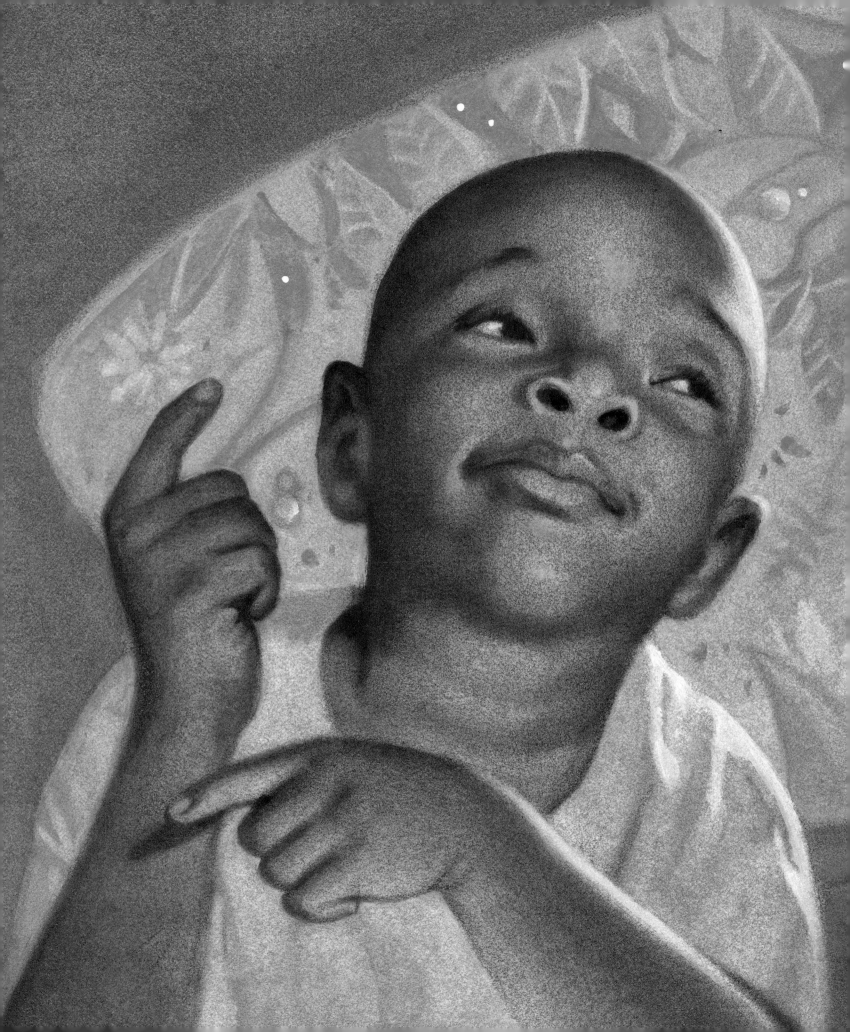

Max giggled as he watched the beautiful bright orb
flicker through the passing trees, trailing behind the car as
it traveled home, this way and that, playing peekaboo.

Up a hill, down a hill, the moon
was ever there. Over a bridge, around
a curve, the moon bounced along!

Around a tree, past a field of
sleeping cows, the moon stayed
quietly with Max.

Through a small town with
roundabout streets, Max gazed
as the moon kept up.

At the mouth of a tunnel and out
the other end, Max smiled when
he saw the moon there, waiting.

Dark clouds tumbled across
the night sky. The stars and
nightingales all faded away.

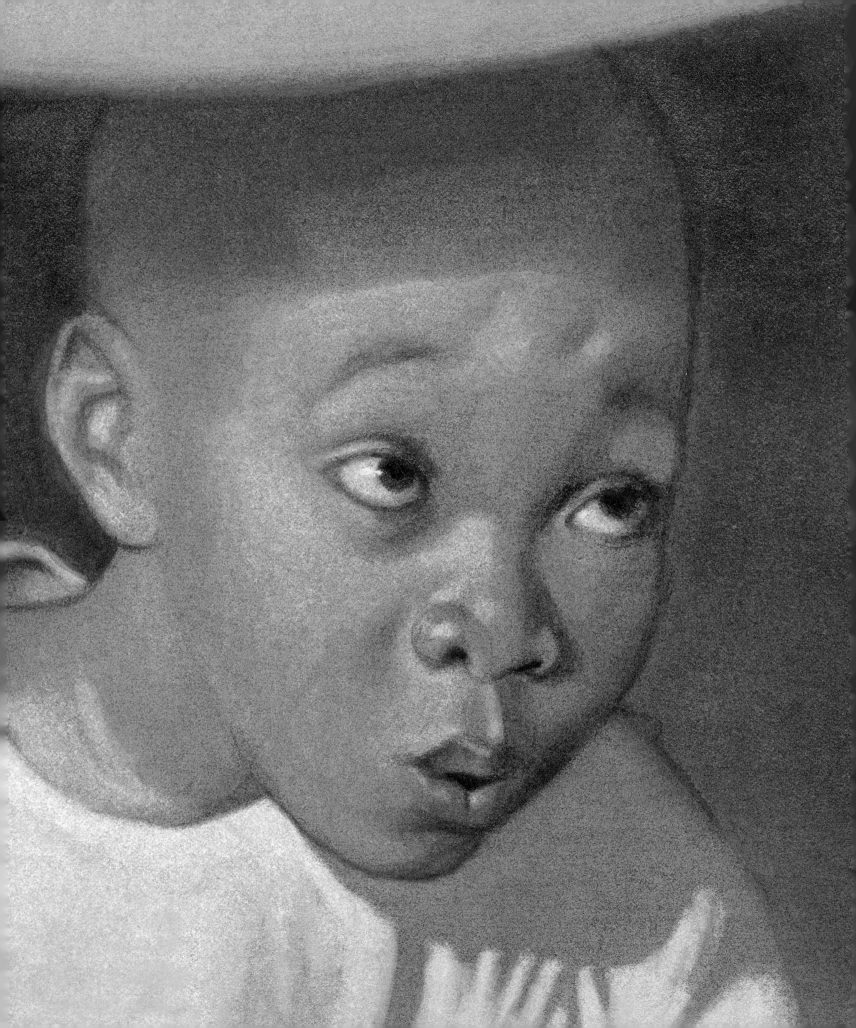

Max searched the darkness and
wondered, where is the moon?
Granpa said it would always shine
for me.

Finally home, Max took one last look
up at the empty night sky.
   "I guess that ol' moon couldn't shine
for me all the way home."

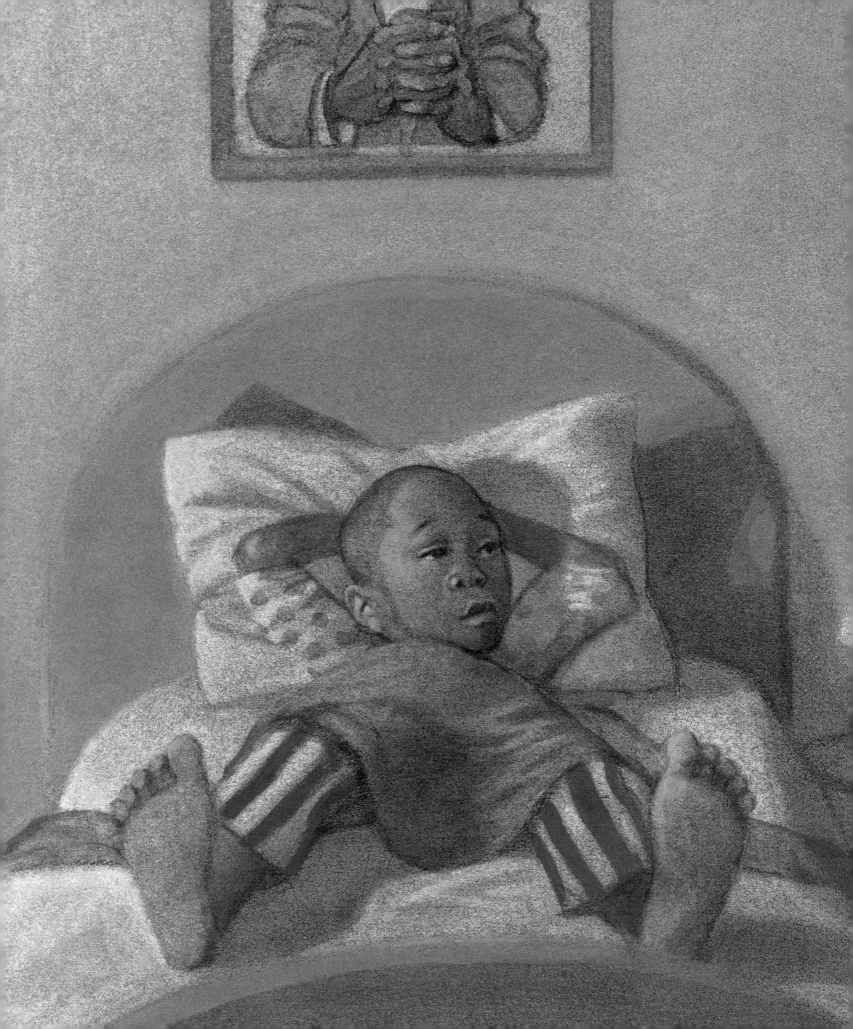

Upstairs in bed, the room
was dark. Max felt alone. He
missed Granpa. He missed that
tag-along moon.

Then slowly, very slowly, Max's bedroom began to fill with a soft yellow glow. The clouds faded away and the moon peeked through!

Max gazed up at that magic ball of light
and thought about what Granpa said.
"That ol' moon will always shine
for me . . . on and on!"

Max knew then that whenever he saw the moon,
he would think of Granpa, on and on.
And he slept soundly, embraced in soft yellow light.